TOM AND THE PTEROSAUR

JENNY NIMMO

Illustrations by
MICHAEL FOREMAN

WALKER BOOKS
AND SUBSIDIARIES

LONDON • BOSTON • SYDNEY

for Jonathan

TOM AND THE PTEROSAUR

TOM DISCOVERS HIS NEXT-DOOR NEIGHBOURS ARE HIDING A SECRET THAT'S BEYOND HIS WILDEST IMAGININGS.

Jenny Nimmo worked at the BBC for a number of years, ending in a spell as a director/adaptor for *Jackanory*. Her many books for children include *Ronnie and the Giant Millipede*, *The Stone Mouse* (shortlisted for the Carnegie Medal and broadcast on BBC TV), *The Owl-tree* (Winner of the 1997 Smarties Book Prize), *Toby in the Dark* and *Dog Star*. Her well-known trilogy, comprising *The Snow Spider* (Winner of the 1986 Smarties Book Prize), *Emlyn's Moon* and *The Chestnut Soldier*, has been made into a TV series. Jenny Nimmo lives in a converted water mill in Wales with her artist husband and, occasionally, her three grown-up children.

First published 2001 by Walker Books Ltd
87 Vauxhall Walk, London SE11 5HJ

2 4 6 8 10 9 7 5 3 1

Text © 2001 Jenny Nimmo
Illustrations © 2001 Michael Foreman

This book has been typeset in Galliard

Printed and bound in Great Britain
by The Guernsey Press Co. Ltd

British Library Cataloguing in Publication Data:
a catalogue record for this book
is available from the British Library

ISBN 0-7445-4178-6

CHAPTER ONE

Tom Tuttle had five sisters. To make matters worse, every one of Tom's sisters sang – nearly all the time. Even the baby, Tilly, followed along when the others were tra-la-la-ing round the house.

Tom's sisters were called Tamara, Tracy, Tabitha, Tulip and Tilly. Tom and Tabitha were twins, though you'd never guess it. Tom couldn't sing a note. The Tuttle sisters thought that one day they would be famous. They decided to call themselves the Tuttle Band. Tom couldn't be part of it. He wasn't musical.

Mr and Mrs Tuttle were very proud of their daughters. They gave Tamara a violin for her eleventh birthday, and when the noise filled the house and shook the walls they only said, "Well done! Keep it up!"

In November, when his sisters started practising their Christmas carols, Tom thought the roof would fall in. Luckily the Tuttles lived in the country, far away from most human beings. Beyond the hill in front of their house a wild sea lashed the cliffs, and seagulls swung through the wind. The Tuttles' only neighbours were the Grimleys, and they never complained about noise. In fact, they were seldom seen.

From their upstairs windows the Tuttles could see a greeny-grey roof and two crooked chimneys. That was all that could be glimpsed of the Grimleys' crumbling old house, even though it was just at the end of the Tuttles' garden. The Grimleys had grown a giant-sized hedge on their side of the fence. It was so tall and so thick, not one tiny thread of light could get through it.

Once, the Grimleys had been friendly. Tom used to go and talk to Mrs Grimley while she fed her animals. She had goats and chickens, two ducks and a donkey called Iris. Sometimes Tom was allowed to ride Iris. And then, one day, something happened. In just a few moments, friendly Mrs Grimley had turned into quite another sort of person: mean, snappy and cold.

"Go away!" she had snarled. "Go on. Go home. And don't come back."

Tom was so shocked he ran away as fast as he could! He climbed over the rickety fence and rushed back to the house that was full of songs. And, for once, he didn't mind all the noise. It made him feel safe. He wanted to tell his sisters about Mrs Grimley turning into a kind of witch, but they were too busy singing. His mum was trying to remember where she'd put the washing (she was a very forgetful person) and Tom could see she wasn't interested. So in the end Tom told his dad, who listened to him and then said, "Tom, don't tell stories." Mr Tuttle was a reporter on the local newspaper, and he was a stickler for the truth.

That very afternoon the Grimleys had put up a new fence, and the next day the trees for the hedge arrived; they were trees that seemed to grow before your very eyes. In two years the hedge was as high as a house. It didn't seem to bother any of the Tuttles, however, except for Tom.

"People want to be private for all sorts of reasons," Mrs Tuttle told him.

Tamara said that Mrs Grimley probably wanted to sunbathe without any clothes on. Tracy said they were probably hiding gangsters. Tabitha thought Mr Grimley could be building a secret weapon; after all, no one knew exactly what he did for a living. Mr Tuttle told them that Mr Grimley was a pensioner, and pensioners didn't build secret weapons.

Mrs Tuttle said, "You never know."

Tom missed his rides on Iris. He missed feeding the ducks and chickens and goats. He had nowhere to run to when his sisters started singing.

To make up for not being musical, Tom started to tell stories. They were mostly about dinosaurs. Tom knew a great deal about dinosaurs. He told his stories to Tilly because she had more time to listen than the others. The trouble was, Tilly believed Tom's stories, he made them sound so real. In fact, he almost believed them himself.

Tilly's favourite story was the one about the tyrannosaurus; Tom said that he'd seen one rampaging round London when he was on a school trip. She also liked the story of the giant bones in the wood, and the one about the diplodocus-dropping in the playground (Tom brought some of it back in his sandwich box). That was when Mr Tuttle put his foot down.

"Tom, you must stop telling stories to Tilly," Mr Tuttle said. "She believes them and they're not true."

"They make her happy," said Tom.

"*That's* true," said Mrs Tuttle.

Encouraged by his mum's remark, Tom

said, "Sometimes my stories help Tilly to sleep. She just nods off with a smile on her face."

"Don't argue," said Mr Tuttle.

But Tom couldn't stop telling stories. It had become a habit, as bad as Mrs Tuttle's habit of forgetting things or Mr Tuttle needing three spoons of sugar in his tea or Tamara's nail-biting or Tracy's hair-sucking. Tom tried to obey his dad by making his stories sound less real, but Tilly still believed them.

At the moment, Tilly was Tom's favourite sister. Tabitha should have been his favourite because she was his twin, but it was Tilly who listened to him, not Tabitha. Besides, Tabitha told on him.

One day, at teatime, Tabitha told their dad that Tom had been given detention.

"So what did you do wrong?" Mr Tuttle asked Tom.

Tom reckoned it would be best to tell the truth. Anyway, he couldn't think of another story quickly enough.

"I thought I saw a stegosaurus's footprint on the football pitch," Tom said in a rush. "I went back to get my ruler to measure it and I missed assembly."

"Tom, you couldn't have seen a stegosaurus's footprint," Mr Tuttle said sternly. "They died out millions of years ago."

"Perhaps it was an elephant's footprint, then," said Tom.

"Stop telling stories!" retorted Mr Tuttle.

Tamara said, "I expect it was a squashed molehill," and she began to sing. *"Away in a manger..."*

Tom noticed that the girls were never told to stop singing. He felt cross and fed up, so he pushed his plate away and left the kitchen. The singing followed him all through the house, wherever he went. He ran out into the garden, right to the very end, to the place where vegetables were supposed to grow but rarely did. It was cold and dark but at least it was quiet.

Beyond the tangled weeds rose the Grimleys' lofty hedge, as tall and solid as the wall of a castle. Tom stared up at it, and for the hundredth time he wondered what had happened to Mrs Grimley. What had changed her? Why couldn't he ride Iris, or feed the goats and chickens?

"AAAK!"

From the other side of the hedge came an eerie shriek. It was an echoey, indoor sort of sound and it made Tom shiver.

"AAAK! AAAK! AAAK!"

Tom thought that Mrs Grimley kept her chickens in the barn behind the hedge, but this wasn't the friendly cluck of a chicken, this cry was desperate and rather lonely. It went on and on and on, the sound of something lost.

"Tom, what are you doing out there?" Mr Tuttle was standing on the back step, and through the open door the girls' voices came pouring into the night.

"The holly and the ivy,
When they are both full grown
Of all the trees that are in the wood,
The holly bears the crown..."

The strange shrieking stopped. It was as if the singing had soothed it somehow. Like a baby being crooned to sleep, like telling stories to Tilly.

Tom wanted to tell his dad about the eerie cries, but he knew Mr Tuttle wouldn't think they were peculiar, even if he heard them.

CHAPTER TWO

Next morning the postman delivered a very unusual letter to Mr Tuttle. The envelope was edged in gold, and the name and address were printed in fruity-coloured letters.

"Looks like you've won something, Mr Tuttle," said the postman.

The Tuttle children crowded round. "Open it, Dad!" they cried. "Quickly! It could be a million pounds!"

It wasn't a million pounds, but to Mr Tuttle it was almost as good. He'd been sponsored by the firm of Fruity Chocs to write about the Amazon jungle. Would he be ready to fly out to Brazil next week?

Mr Tuttle looked at Mrs Tuttle. "Can you manage without me, Audrey?" he asked.

"Course," she said. "Go on, Frank. It's brilliant. You've always wanted to write about the jungle. Take some photos for us."

"Take a video camera," cried Tamara. "Get someone to film you!"

"Our dad in the jungle!" said Tulip. "We can show them at school."

"Will we get loads of Fruity Chocs?" asked Tracy, whose favourite thing was food.

"We three kings ..." sang Tabitha.

"... from Orient are..." went on Tamara.

"He's not going to the Orient; he's going to the Amazon," said Tom.

The girls took no notice. They just went on singing.

The next few days were so taken up with the hustle and bustle of Mr Tuttle's jungle trip, Tom forgot about the mysterious calls from the Grimleys' barn.

On the night before Mr Tuttle's departure, the family had what Mrs Tuttle called an adventurer's feast. She'd been experimenting a bit, so no one really knew what they were eating. But it tasted good. Tracy had three helpings. The girls began to talk about the things that Mr Tuttle might see: the tree frogs, the wild pigs and rainbow-coloured birds.

"I wonder if they sing," said Tabitha.

"The pigs?" asked Tracy.

"The birds, silly!" said Tabitha.

"Beautiful birds don't always sing," Mrs Tuttle told them.

For some reason Tom thought of the calls from the Grimleys' barn. He slipped away from the table and went down to the looming hedge. All he could hear were the sounds of his chattering family and the hum of traffic on a distant motorway.

And then it came. "AAAK! AAAK! AAAK!"

It sounded like a creature from another world. The barn was big enough for a dinosaur, but, of course, Tom knew that dinosaurs were extinct.

"AAAK! AAAK! AAAK!"

The cries were getting fast and desperate,

and Tom thought, Perhaps it's hungry, whatever it is.

At that moment Mrs Tuttle opened the kitchen window. The heat and steam of her exotic cooking was getting too much for her. A burst of singing drifted across the garden.

"My bonnie lies over the ocean,
My bonnie lies over the sea..."

The frantic calls from the barn died to a gentle twitter, and then fell silent.

Tom wished he could tell someone. He wanted to share the mystery of the voice that fell silent when the girls began to sing. Perhaps Tilly would like to hear it.

Tom ran back to the house. The girls were still singing, but Tilly was looking a bit drowsy. Tom took her hand and whispered, "Come with me. There's something I want you to hear."

"What is it?" Tilly suddenly looked wide awake.

"Something special, maybe a dinosaur."

"Oooo!"

Tilly slipped off her chair and together they walked out of the hot singing kitchen. The girls were in full swing now, their voices drowning out every other sound. They were gathered round the sink, Tamara scrubbing dirty saucepans and the others drying and stacking.

"It's your turn to dry, Tom," sang Tamara, still in tune.

Tom pretended not to hear her. He began to run, Tilly's hand clutched tightly in his. They were halfway down the garden when a voice said, "Tom, what are you up to?"

Tom turned to see his dad standing on the back step.

"I ... I just wanted Tilly to hear something," he said. "It's in the Grimleys' barn."

"A dinosaur," said Tilly.

Tom wished she hadn't said that, but it was too late now.

"Come here!" Mr Tuttle's voice was deep and stern.

Tom trudged back to his father with Tilly still clinging to his hand.

"I want to hear the dinosaur," she grumbled.

"There are no dinosaurs," Mr Tuttle said grimly. He told Tilly to go back to the kitchen while he and Tom had a "little chat" in the living-room.

Mr Tuttle didn't sit in his usual armchair. For a long time he stood with his back to the door, just staring at Tom. Tom began to feel quite scared, and then his dad said, "Listen, Tom. Tomorrow I'm going far away. Your mum will be very busy, so you've got to be more helpful."

"How?"

"I know you can't help it, Tom, but you must stop telling stories. Stop inventing things and leading Tilly astray."

"But..." Tom wished his dad had heard the mysterious sounds. "There *is* something peculiar in the Grimleys' barn," he said.

"There *isn't*," said Mr Tuttle. "Now

promise me you won't tell any more stories."

Tom wished his dad could bring himself to believe in extraordinary things, but Mr Tuttle was just not made that way, so with a big sigh Tom said, "I promise." And then he realized that he wouldn't mind not telling stories, because there was a truth, just as strange as all the stories he invented, hidden at the bottom of the garden. Tom had just thought of a way to find out what it was.

CHAPTER THREE

Mr Tuttle's departure was a very grand occasion. The director of Fruity Chocs himself came to shake Mr Tuttle's hand, and the whole family was photographed standing in front of the house. Unfortunately Mrs Tuttle had washed everyone's best clothes the day before and forgotten to iron them, so they looked a bit creased. But Mr Tuttle was the star, so it didn't really matter. He always ironed his own clothes. He'd also packed his own case. He knew Mrs Tuttle would forget something vital, like his toothbrush or his shaving kit. However, he needn't have bothered. The director of Fruity Chocs made him put everything in a brightly coloured rucksack with FRUITY CHOCS printed all over it.

A fruity-coloured limo rolled up. More photographs. Mr Tuttle was whisked into the limo. The family waved. Another photograph. Mrs Tuttle wiped a tear from her cheek. (No photograph of that. This was not supposed to be a sad occasion.) The director, reporter, photographer and other members of the team climbed in beside Mr Tuttle, who was lost in a sea of heads, hats and cameras. The limo drove away.

The Tuttles heaved a sigh of relief and sadness, and Tom rushed upstairs to find his father's binoculars. He was about to put his plan into action.

With the binoculars hanging under his jacket, Tom ran to the garage. He found what he was looking for leaning beside a stack of old spades: the stepladder. Tom dragged the stepladder down to the bottom of the garden. There was no one to ask what he was doing. The girls were busy ironing their clothes, and Mrs Tuttle was trying to remember where she'd put her shopping.

Tom stood the ladder against the fence and climbed to the top. So far so good. Unfortunately the hedge rose several feet above the fence, so he had to make a hole in the thick foliage. After snipping off a few twigs, he managed to push the binoculars into a gap where he could get a good view of the Grimleys' backyard.

The huge barn stood right beside the hedge, but Tom could see past it to the house, on the other side of the yard. Mr Grimley's car was parked in front of the back door. Tom noticed that the chickens now had a brand-new henhouse in the field beyond the yard.

It was amazing how close everything swam when Tom looked through the binoculars. He could see Mr Grimley opening the boot of his car. He could even see what was in the boot: hundreds of cans, all the same size and colour. Whoops! Mr Grimley dropped a can.

Tom focused on the runaway can. He could actually read the print on the side. JUMP it said. FOR TOP DOGS. Just to prove what Jump could do, there was a picture of a jumping dog on the label. The Grimleys didn't have a dog. They didn't even have a cat. So who or what was going to eat hundreds of cans of Jump?

Perhaps the Grimleys make Jump pie every day, Tom thought. He must have spoken his thoughts aloud, because Mr Grimley suddenly stared at the hedge. He was a tall, stringy man with mean little eyes and not very much hair. Tom held the binoculars steady, hardly daring to breathe. As soon as Mr Grimley turned back to the cans, Tom pulled himself out of the hedge and raced down the ladder. His feet had hardly touched the ground when he heard a terrible shriek from the barn. Then another.

"Be quiet," snarled Mr Grimley on the other side of the hedge. "It's coming."

What was coming? Jump pie?

Tom had to see what was going on. Once again he climbed the ladder, poked the binoculars into the hedge and peered through them.

"AAAK!" shrieked the thing in the barn. "AAAK! AAAK! AAAK!"

"Out of this world," Tom breathed. "That's what it is. Out of this world."

"Tom, what are you doing?"

Tom nearly fell. He hadn't expected to hear a voice so close to his feet. Pulling his head out of the hedge, he found Tabitha frowning up at him.

"AAAK!" The shriek from the barn came again. Eerie and frantic.

"Whatever's that?" said Tabitha.

"I don't know," whispered Tom. "Tabitha, will you do something for me?"

"Depends," said his sister carefully. "Why are you whispering?"

"I don't want next door to know I'm here," Tom explained. "Do you mind singing something?"

"Course not," said Tabitha. "I never mind singing. But next door will know we're here if I sing, won't they?"

"Erm..." Tom hadn't thought of that. He

climbed down the ladder.

The next minute there was a series of such horrible sounds that the twins had to cover their ears with their hands.

"Sing now, Tabs!" Tom shouted.

Tabitha liked a bit of a stage. She climbed the ladder and when she was almost at the top, she turned, swept out one hand, and began:

> *"In the bleak midwinter*
> *Frosty wind made moan..."*

Tom wished his twin had chosen something more cheerful. Nevertheless he urged her on. "Go on! Go on!"

> *"Earth stood hard as iron,*
> *Water like a stone;*
> *Snow had fallen, snow on snow..."*

The shrieking died to a murmur and then stopped altogether as Tabitha's voice rang into the frosty air.

"In the bleak midwinter,
Lo–o–ong ago."

"You can stop now," Tom said.

But Tabitha was in no mood to stop. Tom had to wait for another two verses before the carol petered out. By then, much to his surprise, he was beginning to enjoy his sister's singing. Closing his eyes, he could almost feel snowflakes brushing his cheek; he could almost imagine iron-hard ground beneath his feet, and see a block of water, frozen like a stone.

"The thing's gone quiet," said Tabitha. "Whatever it is!"

"It does that when it hears singing," said Tom.

"I wonder if the Grimleys heard me?" Tabitha peeped through the hedge. "Wow!" she said in a hushed voice.

"What? What?" Tom whispered urgently.

"Really weird," said Tabitha.

"What *is* it? Tell me!"

"I think you'd better see."

Tabitha climbed down, and Tom leapt to take her place. He didn't need binoculars to see what his sister had found so weird.

Marching across the Grimleys' backyard was what appeared to be Mrs Grimley. She wore a cycle helmet, thick leather gauntlets, motorcycle goggles, a very long coat and stout leather boots. In one hand she carried a bucket and, as she came closer to the hedge, Tom could see what was in it. It looked like dog food.

When Mrs Grimley reached the barn door, she put down the bucket and drew back two huge bolts. Pulling the door ajar, she peered inside.

"Where are you, my lovely?" she called.

For a moment there was silence, and then a sound like a great sigh could be heard. Mrs Grimley swung the bucket through the door. There was a shriek and a bang.

And Mrs Grimley screamed.

CHAPTER FOUR

Tom wobbled so violently his feet slipped off the ladder and he tumbled to the ground.

"What happened?" said Tabitha, helping Tom to his feet.

"The thing must have attacked Mrs Grimley. She probably wears all that stuff to protect herself."

"Shall we tell someone?" asked Tabitha.

"No. Not yet. Let's find out what it is." Tom sat on one of the steps and rubbed his sore knees.

"OK," said Tabitha. "It'll be our secret."

"And Tilly's," said Tom. "She sort of knows."

Tom had never shared a secret with his twin. It was good to know that someone else had heard the "thing" next door. At last he could have a serious talk about it.

"D'you remember when Mrs Grimley turned horrible?" he asked Tabitha. "I saw it happen. One minute she was OK, then, pouf, she was snarling. And the next day they put the trees in for the hedge. Remember?"

Tabitha shook her head. "Not really."

Tom sighed. "No, you were probably singing."

"So? What's wrong with singing?" Tabitha said hotly. "You're like everyone else, teasing us and laughing at us and being mean, and calling me Tabby the yowler."

Tom was astonished. "Who says that?"

"Everyone. Well, mostly the girls at school. Haven't you noticed?"

"No. Anyway, you've got a lovely voice."

It was Tabitha's turn to look surprised. "Have I?"

"You know you have."

"Yes, I suppose I do. I'm just surprised. You've never said anything nice to me before."

"Haven't I?"

Tom stared at his twin for a moment, then, without a word, he stood up and began to walk back to the house. Tabitha walked beside him, not even singing. But just before they went inside she said, "You must know why Mrs Grimley turned funny. You were there. Try and remember what happened. I bet it's got something to do with the thing."

Tom took his sister's advice. He sat in his room and tried to remember every detail of the strange day when Mrs Grimley turned peculiar. He had gone to give Iris a carrot. He was in the yard, stroking the donkey, when Mrs Grimley came round the side of the house with a bucket of corn. She didn't see Tom. She opened the barn door and out came the hens. And something else!

It was very big, that something else. It had bony grey wings and a long beak. It couldn't walk very well.

"What's that?" Tom had asked, pointing at the strange bird thing.

Mrs Grimley swung round. "What are you doing here?" she said.

"I came to see Iris. What's that big ... thing?"

"A turkey," said Mrs Grimley.

"No it's not," said Tom. "I've seen a turkey before."

That was the moment. Exactly then. Mrs Grimley's face went a ghostly white. Her eyes goggled and her mouth sagged. "Go away!" she snarled. "Go on. Go home. And don't come back."

Tom went. The only time he'd tried to see Iris again, Mr Grimley was in the yard. He shouted at Tom and chased him away.

Tom thought, I saw the thing when it was a baby. But it's grown and grown and now it's a giant thing. And the Grimleys don't want anyone to know.

At teatime Tom leant close to Tabitha and whispered, "I've remembered something."

"Tell me," she whispered back.

"What are you two whispering about?" asked Tamara.

"It's a secret," said Tabitha.

"Oh? Since when have you two had secrets?" Tamara demanded.

"Since today," Tabitha told their oldest sister.

For a moment Tamara looked taken aback, and then she said, "And why, may I ask, is the stepladder at the bottom of the garden? Is that part of the secret?" Tamara could be very severe.

Thinking quickly, Tom said, "I lost a ball and I thought it might be next door, so I got the ladder to look over the fence."

"And through the hedge," added Tabitha.

"How peculiar," Tracy remarked. "Why don't you just go round and ask?"

"I can't *talk* to the Grimleys," Tom said, aghast. "No one can. They don't like visitors. Do they, Mum?"

"I don't know," said Mrs Tuttle. "Mind you, when I forgot to buy sugar, I went round to borrow some and they were very unfriendly. No," she said thoughtfully, "I wouldn't go round there if I were you, Tom."

Tom had just decided that was exactly what he would do. After tea he took Tabitha into the garden to play football. He dribbled the ball to the end of the garden and said, "I'm going to throw the ball over the hedge."

"Why?" asked Tabitha.

"So that if I'm caught next door, I can say I came to fetch my ball."

Tabitha stared at her brother. "Are you going to see the thing?"

"I'm going to try."

"I'll stay here in case you need me," she said.

Tom took out his torch and, feeling a bit like Jack the giant-killer, marched round the house and out into the lane. Dusk had brought an icy mist drifting through the trees, and Tom found that his torch was no use. He had to feel his way, step by step, round the sharp bend in the lane and then on to the Grimleys' front gate. Their second gate was heavy and difficult to open. Tom climbed over it.

Now he was on the drive that led round the Grimleys' house and into the yard. A slither of light crept past the curtains in the front room, but the back of the house was dark and silent. Tom tiptoed slowly across the yard. He could see his white football lying in front of the barn.

With one eye on the Grimleys' back door, Tom ran over to the barn. The bolts on the door looked old and stiff. There was one at the bottom and one just above his head. Slowly, and with some difficulty, he managed to tug back the big, rusty bolts.

There was no going back. Tom pulled the barn door open, just a crack, slid inside and closed the door behind him. The smell was terrible, worse than a cowshed. Nothing could be seen. It was like being blind. He didn't dare shine his torch in case he alarmed the thing. He listened for sounds. Nothing, until...

A board creaked somewhere, and the dust inside the barn was stirred into a swirling breeze. A cloud of grit and hayseed flew into Tom's face as something huge swept towards him through the air.

CHAPTER FIVE

Tom fell to his knees, burying his face in his hands.

He hadn't thought about what would happen if he met the thing. He hadn't wondered about how big the thing was – or if it ate people. Crouched in the dark, Tom's fearful imagining created something so dreadful he could hardly breathe. He only needed the courage to open the barn door and crawl away, but he couldn't move. And then his terrible situation became very much worse. The thing began to cry.

A lost and desperate wail drifted round the barn as great wings churned the air, beating against the walls and rafters. And yet, even while Tom silently begged the thing to stop, he felt the dreadful voice was telling him not to be afraid, that it was lost and lonely, and only wanted to be where it belonged.

But Tom *was* afraid. He couldn't help it. And then he remembered that Tabitha was on the other side of the hedge. "In case you need me," she had said. Tom had heard that sometimes twins were born with magic between them and could read each other's thoughts.

The creature was becoming more desperate; its cries rose to a piercing shriek.

Sing, Tabitha! Sing! Tom sent his silent message. *Sing! Sing! Sing!* Tom imagined his thoughts to be like tiny stars, floating through the night, over the hedge and down onto Tabitha's outstretched fingers.

And Tabitha answered; clear as a bell, her voice came ringing through the darkness.

"It came upon the midnight clear,
That glorious song of old,
From angels bending near the earth
To touch their harps of gold..."

The creature grew hesitant. "Aaak!" it called sadly. "Aaak!"

"*The world in solemn stillness lay,*" sang Tabitha, "*To hear the angels sing.*"

The frantic wails died to a murmur. Somewhere in the dark two great wings were slowly folding, glinting eyes were closing, a giant beak drooping, as the creature listened to Tabitha's voice.

> "*Still through the cloven skies they come,*
> *With peaceful wings unfurled;*
> *And still their heavenly music floats*
> *O'er all the weary world...*"

The barn was silent. Nothing stirred. Tom should have backed out then, through the door, but, much to his surprise, he found himself walking forward into the deep stillness of the barn. As he moved, the utter darkness began to lift a little, and he could make out the wide beams above his head and the pale straw scattered round his feet.

Almost before he knew it Tom had reached the last beam, and there it was. He had never been so close to anything as huge and strange as the creature above him. It loomed over him, its great wings folded into angles as sharp as swords, its inky talons hooked against the beam. But the head, with its dreadful beak, drooped sleepily, and Tom wasn't afraid.

It knows I'm here, he thought, and he had the oddest feeling that the lonely creature was glad he was there. So he stood as close as he could, and whispered, "I know what you are, even if it's impossible, even if no one ever believes me. I know that you are a pterosaur. I know that you should be living with dinosaurs two hundred million years ago. But you're not. And I don't know what I can do about that."

Tom turned and crept away. He slipped through the barn door and closed it softly. But just as he was pushing the last bolt into place a gruff voice called, "Who's there?"

Tom stiffened. Tabitha, hearing Mr

Grimley's voice, raised her own in a wonderful crescendo.

"Shut that racket!" yelled tone-deaf Mr Grimley.

Safely shrouded in mist, Tom shouted, "It's not a racket. It's a Christmas carol." He scooped up his football, raced across the yard, and climbed over the gate before Mr Grimley had time to work out where he was.

Tabitha was perched on the stepladder when Tom found her. "Did you see it?" she asked. "What's it like? Did the singing help?"

"You sent it to sleep," Tom told her. "It's a pterosaur."

"A what?"

"A flying dinosaur."

Tabitha stared at him before slowly descending the ladder. "But..." she began.

"I know what you're going to say. They're extinct. Well, this one isn't." Tom's voice was so solemn, Tabitha couldn't argue.

"Wow!" she said. "What shall we do?"

"Nothing."

"But we ought to tell the newspapers!" Tabitha exclaimed. "It'll be famous. It'll be on the telly."

"I don't think it wants to be famous," said Tom.

"Oh." Tabitha looked disappointed.

"Two amazing things happened today," Tom said quickly. "One, I saw a pterosaur, and two, I discovered we've got telepathy."

"What's that?" Tabitha asked suspiciously.

"We can read each other's thoughts. I wanted you to sing, to make the pterosaur quiet, and you did."

"I sang because the thing was making such a noise, and singing worked before; I didn't read your thoughts."

"Oh." It was Tom's turn to be disappointed.

When they got back to the house, Mrs Tuttle popped out of the kitchen and said, "Before I forget, Tom, Mrs Grimley has just phoned. She says if you go into their yard again it'll ... it'll..."

Tamara poked her head round the door, and filled in the bit that her mum had forgotten. "It'll be the worse for you."

Tom wondered what Mrs Grimley would do if he went into her yard. It wasn't as if she was a real witch and could make him disappear. Or could she? He decided not to test her – yet.

Next day Tabitha was swept into rehearsals for the school concert. She didn't have time to discuss things any more. For a week the girls had to stay behind after school. They learnt new carols, and new ways of singing them. Mrs Foley, the music teacher, brought them home every day and always stayed for a cup of tea.

One day Mrs Foley said, "You know, Mrs Tuttle, your girls are truly gifted. I hope they remember their old music teacher when they're famous."

"Of course they will," said Mrs Tuttle, who couldn't remember where she'd put the teapot.

Tom tried to put the pterosaur out of his mind for a while, but Tilly kept asking for stories about it. She got quite sulky when he couldn't find anything to say. Stories were easy, but when there was a real creature, trapped in a barn in the wrong part of time, it didn't seem right to make up a story about it. Stories had to be funny or scary, and they had to have happy endings. Tom didn't see how the pterosaur could have a happy ending. Unless...

CHAPTER SIX

Ten days after Mr Tuttle had left for his Amazon adventure, two postcards arrived from him. Mrs Tuttle's card had a picture of trees and monkeys on the front, the children's had a chameleon. The chameleon was quite hard to make out because it was almost the same colour as the branch it was sitting on.

On the back of the children's card Mr Tuttle had written:

There's so much I want to tell you, but it'll have to wait until I get back. It wouldn't all fit on this card. Children, I'm beginning to believe there are things in this world that no one will ever understand. I miss you all.
Love from your dad xxxxx

Those weren't at all the sort of words the dad Tom knew would have used. Mr Tuttle had always made it his business to understand *everything*. Tom wondered what had happened to his dad out there in the jungle.

Mrs Tuttle's card explained a bit more. "Your dad says he's met some Indians," she told the children, "and a medicine man who ... who..." she brought the card closer to her nose and read it aloud, "'who can summon up spirits. Audrey, I'm beginning to believe in the impossible. Me, of all people.'" Mrs Tuttle put the card down. "Well," she said. "Who'd have thought it?"

While Mr Tuttle was steaming in the jungle, his family was piling on blankets and muffling up in woolly hats and scarves. A hard white frost covered the fields, and even the trees were hung with icicles. Earth was indeed as hard as iron. And then the snow began to fall. Snow on snow.

Tom hadn't heard the pterosaur for over a week. He was uneasy. From his spyhole in the hedge he could see a deserted yard. The water trough was covered with a thick sheet of ice. A bucket had blown onto its side, the water inside it frozen solid. All the curtains in the Grimleys' house were drawn across. Could they have left home? And, if they had, what had become of their animals? Tom decided to find out.

Next morning he pleaded a sore throat. "I'b cubig dowd wib subthig, bub," he told his mother in a pretend coldy voice.

"You'd better stay indoors today," said Mrs Tuttle.

When the girls went to school, Tom was left behind, but he didn't intend to stay indoors. After breakfast he slipped a carrot and a tin of sardines into his pocket. Why the sardines? Tom would have said it was his sixth sense.

As soon as Mrs Tuttle started her washing-machine, Tom put on his anorak, pulled on his wellies and stepped out into the icy air. CRUNCH! CRUNCH! He plodded through the snow and out into the lane. The Grimleys' gate was rimed with frost. Tom gasped as his fingers met the icy bars. He'd forgotten his gloves. He swung himself over the gate and thumped into the snow on the other side.

The yard was utterly silent. Mr Grimley's car, covered in snow, stood by the back door. There were no footprints, no tyre marks across the frozen yard.

Tom found Iris in the lean-to beside the barn. She brayed with delight when she saw Tom. "Hee-haw! Hee-haw! Hee-haw!" But the Grimleys' curtains didn't move.

Tom gave Iris the carrot and moved a bale of hay into her shelter. Then he took a spade and cracked the ice in the water trough. He filled a bucket with water and took it to Iris. By this time the chickens were calling from the henhouse. Tom found a sack of corn and scattered some of it on the floor. The ducks appeared to have flown away and the goats were happily nibbling things in the vegetable plot. There was only one thing left to do.

The bolts on the barn door were swollen

with frost. Tom couldn't budge them. Again and again he blew on his freezing fingers, but his hands were numb with cold. He searched the yard and, beside a pile of logs, found a hammer.

CLANG! CLANG! CLANG! Tom hammered at the frozen bolts and, at last, they began to move. But the deafening blows made no impression on the Grimleys. Nothing stirred in the old house.

The second bolt slid back and the frozen door shivered open. Tom stepped into the barn. He'd been too nervous to notice the smell before, but now it hit him. The fierce reek of stale air and muck. He opened the door wider to let in fresh air, and then, in the weak shaft of snowy light, he saw it – a dark shape right at the end of the barn. It was perched on a beam, its head drooping between folded wings. Its eyes were closed but the great spoon-shaped beak hung open and, as Tom approached, he could see the rows of treacherous teeth. There was no doubt about what it was. Birds didn't have teeth; their wings were feathery, not great sheets of skin.

"You're in a bad way, aren't you?" said Tom.

A rasping sigh came from the pterosaur.

It needed food and water. It needed sunshine and hope. Tom could supply everything but the sunshine. He found an empty tin bath beside the door and carried it to the trough. When he'd filled the bath with water, he placed it close to the pterosaur's beam. Then he opened the tin of sardines and laid them beside the water.

The pterosaur didn't move. Tom stood as near as he dared and said, "I can't sing, but I'll tell you a story."

He stayed in the barn, talking softly until his voice had all but disappeared, and then he crept away. He didn't bolt the door, but left it open, just wide enough to let in a sunbeam, if any should appear.

Tom didn't tell anyone where he'd been or what he'd done. Not even Tabitha, who began to practise a new song as soon as she came home.

At teatime Mrs Tuttle suddenly slapped a hand to her head and declared, "It's Saturday tomorrow. I nearly forgot! Your dad's coming home. We'll all go shopping, shall we, to buy his favourite food?"

Tom wondered if he could slip a few tins of dog food into the trolley without anyone noticing.

That night the cold north wind did a sort of somersault and turned south. Tom lay awake, listening to the drip, drip of melting ice. In the morning the snow had thawed; it was rushing down the lane in a bubbling stream. The sun was shining and the world was green again.

Tom didn't have a chance to visit the pterosaur because he had to help clean the house and wash the car. At half past five Mrs Tuttle gave a yelp and said, "Quickly, everyone! Into the car. Your dad'll be home at seven. We've just got time to buy the feast."

The children piled uncomfortably into the Tuttles' ancient station wagon and, with groans and grumbles from the back, Mrs Tuttle drove rather dangerously to the supermarket.

They got there ten minutes before closing time. Only one checkout was open. The girl sitting behind it yawned and looked cross when the Tuttles came in.

"Won't be long!" Mrs Tuttle called sweetly. She grabbed a trolley and lifted Tilly into the little seat. Tamara took the list and began to throw things in. It was astonishing how quickly the trolley filled up. They raced round the aisles and managed to reach the grumpy checkout girl with a minute to spare.

"I hope I haven't forgotten anything," said Mrs Tuttle, pushing her trolley through the automatic doors. "It would be—" Her voice came to an abrupt halt at the same time as her trolley.

The Tuttles stared into the carpark, too

amazed to speak.

There was something on top of their station wagon. Something huge. Its giant wings were folded like two tall umbrellas, and one of its talons appeared to have smashed the windscreen.

"A dinosaur," breathed Tilly.

"A *pter*osaur," said the twins.

CHAPTER SEVEN

"It can't be." Mrs Tuttle found her voice at last. "Pterosaurs are extinct."

"Not this one," said Tom. "It comes from next door." He didn't mention the sardines or the door that he'd purposely left open.

"I'll telephone the RSPCA," said Mrs Tuttle, swinging her trolley round. "Or the police – they'll know what to do. There's a phone in the store."

When she approached the automatic doors, however, they wouldn't open. The store was in darkness. Everyone had vanished. Even the carpark was empty – except for the pterosaur.

Tulip began to cry and Tracy whined, "I'm starving. Can I have a biscuit?" She plunged her hand into the trolley, upsetting half its contents.

All at once the pterosaur shook its great wings. "AAAK! AAAK! AAAK!" it called.

Everyone screamed – except Tom.

"It's hungry," he said.

"Well, it's not having your dad's bacon," said Mrs Tuttle. "In fact, it's not having one tiny scrap of our welcome-home feast." And with that she swung her trolley round once more, and headed towards a shadowy gate that led to the back lane.

The children ran after her. "Mum, where are you going?" they cried.

"I'm going to push this trolley all the way home if I have to," panted Mrs Tuttle. "We can't use the car, that's for sure."

As they filed through the gate, Tom looked back. The pterosaur, craning its long neck, was watching them.

The lane was dark, but the lights from passing cars helped a little.

"It's miles," moaned Tracy. "All the frozen stuff will unfreeze."

"Let me push the trolley," said Tamara.

"I can go faster."

"We'll take a short cut through the park," said Mrs Tuttle, handing over the trolley.

"If it's open," muttered Tamara.

Tom felt a tug on his sleeve. "You let it out, didn't you?" whispered Tabitha.

"Yes," Tom whispered, "but I didn't—"

"Why are you two whispering?" demanded Tamara.

"It's a secret," said Tabitha.

Mercifully the park gates were still open. The trolley bumped and squeaked as the Tuttle family pounded over the grass. They were halfway across the green when they felt the air stir and sigh and, looking up, they saw the two great sheets of the pterosaur's wings circling above them.

Everyone screamed again and Mrs Tuttle, forgetting all she'd said about Mr Tuttle's welcome-home feast, cried, "Leave the trolley and run, children. *Run!*"

"Where to?" they cried.

"The bandstand," said their mum. "At least

we'll have a roof."

They raced towards the bandstand with its circle of lights under a pretty painted roof. Then they leapt up the wooden steps and crouched behind the railings.

"It's like a fairy's house," breathed Tulip through her sobs of fright.

They looked out to where the trolley stood in the thin gleam from the bandstand lights. And they gasped.

"Oh, children," cried Mrs Tuttle. "I forgot Tilly!"

There she was, her pale legs swinging from the trolley seat. The pterosaur had landed on a pile of tins at the other end of the trolley. It began to peck at the packaging with its great beak. In a few seconds the dreadful spiked teeth would reach Tilly.

Mrs Tuttle was about to race across the grass, but Tamara and Tracy held her back. "You'll get eaten, Mum!" they yelled.

"Oh, what can we do? What can we do?" wailed Mrs Tuttle.

Almost without thinking, Tom said, *"Sing!"*

"Sing?" said Tamara, as though it were the silliest thing in the world.

"Yes, sing!" Tom repeated. "Singing calms it down. It makes it go kind of sleepy. If you all sing, then I can creep out and rescue Tilly."

"Can you?" Mrs Tuttle was too anxious to ask how Tom knew the creature's habits.

"What shall we sing?" asked Tabitha.

"The carol you sang when I was in the barn," said Tom. "You know, Tabs!"

Everyone looked at Tabitha. Tabitha opened her mouth but no sound came out.

"Come on! *Come on!*" cried Tom. "Night and day you've all been singing, singing, singing. Surely you can manage a few tunes now!"

"Please *try*, girls," said Mrs Tuttle.

Tamara, Tracy, Tabitha and Tulip opened their mouths. What came out was a raggedy, frightened sort of moan.

"Do it properly," commanded Tom. "You've got to start together, and keep the rhythm going." He began to tap the floor with his foot and, before he knew it, found that he was waving his arms about like Mrs Foley, the music teacher.

The girls stared at their brother in amazement. He was conducting. He was keeping time. He had rhythm.

"Tom, you *are* musical!" cried Tabitha.

"Musical boys don't always sing," murmured Mrs Tuttle.

"Girls, concentrate!" said Tom.

They all began to sing.

When the Tuttle Band was singing smoothly, Tom looked over his shoulder. The pterosaur had turned towards the bandstand. Its eyes held a mysterious gleam. No sound came from Tilly. She was gazing intently at the huge creature.

Tom thought, She's not afraid of dinosaurs. She thinks she knows them, because of all those stories I told her. He wondered if he could be as brave as Tilly, and shivered, wishing that he didn't have to run out into the darkness all alone.

"I'm going now," he said. "Keep up the singing."

"I'll come with you," whispered Tabitha. "It'll need two of us."

"OK." Tom grabbed his sister's hand and together they crept down the steps and out onto the shadowy grass.

The pterosaur was motionless. It stared at the bandstand, its gaze never wavering as the twins tiptoed behind it.

"Don't make a sound," Tom whispered to Tilly. "I'm going to lift you out of the trolley."

Without a word, Tilly put her hands on Tom's shoulders. Her eyes were wide and shining. Tom heaved and Tabitha pushed Tilly's feet. Tilly wriggled until she was out of the seat and clinging to Tom's neck. Tom glanced at the pterosaur. It looked like a statue, it was so eerily still. The girls' voices rang out in the cold air.

"The world in solemn stillness lay
To hear the angels sing."

What could that sound mean to an ancient creature? Tom wondered. "Let's go," he whispered.

The twins ran towards the fairy lights. When they had almost reached the bandstand, Mrs Tuttle swooped over to them and gathered Tilly into her arms.

"I'm so sorry," she cried. "I forgot you, Tilly!"

"It's only a dinosaur," said Tilly.

"A *ptero*saur," panted Tom.

The sudden burst of activity had broken the spell. The pterosaur turned away from the singers and began to tear at the packages in the trolley. Out tumbled the sausages, the bacon and several chops.

"There won't be any food left," whined Tracy.

But all at once the great creature stopped eating. Was it sorry that the singing had ended? Whatever it was, the pterosaur decided to abandon the trolley. Spreading its wings, it sailed into the distant shadows.

"Where's it gone?" said Tamara.

"I don't care," said Mrs Tuttle. "I'm going to get that trolley."

"You're joking!" cried Tracy.

Mrs Tuttle wasn't joking. "I've forgotten too many things today," she said, "but I'm not forgetting your dad's feast – what's left of it."

Down the steps she bounded, and out into the dark and dangerous spaces of the park. Seizing her trolley, she ran, ran, ran across the grass while the children raced behind her, Tamara carrying Tilly piggyback. They didn't stop until they reached the gate onto the main road, and even when they were safe on the pavement they kept on running.

CHAPTER EIGHT

Off the main road and down a lane towards their lonely cottage, the Tuttles bumped and clattered in the murky night. Moonlight flitted through the clouds, one moment lighting their way, the next plunging them into inky gloom.

Tom looked up the lane, trying to judge how far they'd have to go. In the distance a light winked on and then another. Tabitha must have seen them too, because suddenly they both said, "Dad's back!" And then, speaking together again, "Let's go and tell him."

They raced up the lane while the lights swam closer. Breathlessly they tore through their own front gate and up to the door, and there Tom stopped.

"How can I tell Dad we're being chased by a pterosaur?" he said. "He won't believe me."

"But it's true," said Tabitha, "and Mum's seen it too." She rang the bell.

A moment later Mr Tuttle was staring out at the twins. "What's going on?" he said, giving them both a hug. "Where are the others?"

Tom took a deep breath. "They're down the lane," he said. "Mum's got what's left of your supper in a supermarket trolley."

His dad looked puzzled. "What's happened to the car? Did Mum forget it?" He laughed at his own joke.

"A pterosaur got it," said Tom. "It ate your supper, too."

"And then it chased us," added Tabitha.

Mr Tuttle's eyebrows made a tiny frown. No more than that. And then he was dashing down the path and out into the lane.

In no time at all Mr Tuttle had wheeled the battered trolley into the house, and soon the tired and hungry family was eating a very tasty dish. Mr Tuttle had come home with some delicious jungle spices (not to mention coloured feathers, rainbow hats, fancy slippers and amazing stories).

Everyone wanted to tell Mr Tuttle about the pterosaur, but Tabitha said, "Let Tom! He knows more than anyone else."

So Tom began on the day he saw the thing that wasn't a turkey waddling out of the Grimleys' barn. And while he spoke he watched his dad's face, waiting for the moment when Mr Tuttle would say, "Don't tell stories, Tom." But the moment never came, and long before he'd finished his story, Tom had come to the conclusion that the jungle had changed Mr Tuttle. It had helped him to believe in the impossible.

"And where's this poor creature now?" asked Mr Tuttle.

The children all had different ideas. While they were arguing Mrs Tuttle heard the doorbell. She slipped away to answer it and came back with a wheezy, white-faced woman. Mrs Grimley.

There was an astonished silence. Everyone gaped at Mrs Grimley.

Coughing and snuffling, the visitor staggered to the table and dropped into Mrs Tuttle's chair. "I've had the flu," she explained. "Both of us. Three days. Knocked us out; we couldn't move. And then this morning when I went to ... went to ... feed the animals it..." She gave a heart-rending moan. "It ... my precious had gone."

"You mean the pterosaur, don't you?" said Tom. "I let it out. It was hungry and it needed sunshine."

"Oh, my treasure," moaned Mrs Grimley.

Mr Tuttle leant across to her. "Where did this thing come from?" he asked.

A strange gleam entered Mrs Grimley's watery eyes. "Well," she said, "I can't really tell you. It was like a dream. We were on holiday in Spain, Mr Grimley and myself, sitting on a lovely sunny beach. We closed our eyes and fell fast asleep, and then something woke me. When I opened my eyes there it was, sitting at my feet – a big, roundish white thing. An egg. It must have come in on the tide, because my toes were all wet. I picked it up and cradled it in my lap – I can't explain why. When Mr Grimley woke up he was most put out. 'Put that down,' he said. 'It doesn't belong to you. It doesn't belong in this world by the look of it.' He thought it would affect me in some way. Well, I suppose it did."

Mrs Grimley blew her nose on a grimy handkerchief, while the silent Tuttles waited expectantly.

"I hid it in my beach towel and brought it home," went on their visitor. Her voice had acquired a deep huskiness that suited the story perfectly. "Mr Grimley disapproved, but I couldn't help myself." She gave a rattling cough. "I never thought it would hatch, but it did. And I loved that skinny bundle more than any creature I've known. I wanted to keep it secret – safe. I wouldn't let Mr Grimley tell a soul. I knew they'd take it away. Put it in a zoo, or a museum. But it grew. It grew and grew and grew."

"We've seen it," said Mrs Tuttle. "It ate our sausages and bacon."

"Ooooo!" wailed Mrs Grimley. "My poor love. He does get cross sometimes. But he's not so bad. He loves music, you know, especially singing. When he was a baby I used to leave the radio on in the barn, to help him sleep, but then he grew and tried to eat it. Oh, what's going to happen to my poor precious?"

"We ought to tell the police it's on the loose," said Tamara.

"No," said Tom. "Not yet. It might come home."

Mrs Grimley smiled across at him. "You're a good boy, Tom," she said.

And so it was decided that nothing should be done until the morning. Mrs Grimley wished the Tuttles goodnight, and Mrs Tuttle promised to take her some nice hot soup later on.

Tom lay awake for a long time. He was

beginning to understand what had happened to Mrs Grimley. She hadn't become a witch. She'd sort of fallen in love with a creature. It had rolled in with the tide and she had caught it. She should have let it go back.

He woke up very early. Even before he reached the window he knew it had been snowing again. The world was so quiet, even the birds were silent. When he looked out, there it was, lying in the garden like a ragged grey blanket. Its wings were covered in snow.

Tom wouldn't let himself believe that it was dead. He raced outside without bothering to find his slippers. His toes stinging with cold, Tom leapt across the icy ground. The pterosaur lay on its side. One golden eye blinked up at the cold sky, but the creature made no sound.

Tom said, "I'll get some food, and maybe a blanket."

The pterosaur was so huge he wondered if he could find anything big enough to cover it. Its flattened wings filled the garden. Perhaps if he gathered up all the coats in the house...

He turned and saw his father standing by the open door.

"It's here!" Tom said. "The pterosaur. It can't get up."

Mr Tuttle stepped towards him. He stared at the pterosaur, lost for words.

"I think the snow is killing it," said Tom. "I'll get some food, shall I? And blankets?"

"Do that, Tom," Mr Tuttle murmured. "And put some shoes on."

Tom ran into the house, flung on his coat and wellies, and then raided the fridge. He carried a tray of food outside and found the rest of his family had crept into the garden. For once they couldn't find anything to say. The creature lying at their feet was so vast, so strange, so very nearly dead.

At last Tilly whispered, "It's like a cloud that's crashed."

Tom spread the food beside the creature's awesome beak. The big head moved. Tom jumped away.

"What's to be done?" said Mrs Tuttle. "D'you think the RSPCA ... or ... or ... the police?"

Mr Tuttle paced the garden, head bent, hands behind his back.

"We'll be famous," said Tamara. "Phone the paper, Dad!"

Tom and Tabitha glanced at each other over a giant wing. "Don't," they said. "Let's keep it secret."

Mr Tuttle looked up with a smile. "I agree with the twins," he said. "Can you imagine this poor creature in a zoo? In a cage? Being examined, gazed at, X-rayed?"

"But, Dad, it might eat people if we let it go," said Tracy.

"I nearly forgot the Grimleys," said Mrs Tuttle. "I'll phone them. After all, it's their responsibility." She ran indoors.

"Look! Look!" cried Tilly, pointing at the pterosaur.

Very slowly the pterosaur's long beak moved towards the food. It scooped up a piece of fish, then another. It crunched an egg, four burgers and a slice of pizza.

"Our lunch!" whined Tracy. "It's..." The twins gave her such a withering look she couldn't go on. "Oh well," she sighed.

"It won't be a secret for long," said Tamara, "filling up our garden like this. Look at it! That big bird will never fly again."

"It's not a bird," said Tom, "and we'll help it to fly, over the sea to somewhere wild. It'll find its way to the place where it belongs."

Easier said than done. The pterosaur's wings were laden with snow. It needed currents of warm air to lift it into the sky, and the only currents available seemed to be freezing.

"Tom," said Mr Tuttle thoughtfully, "fetch the broom. The nice soft one."

Tom ran indoors. When he returned, the Grimleys were standing just inside the gate. They looked old and ill.

"My poor precious." Mrs Grimley gazed lovingly at the pterosaur. "I never thought it would come to this."

"I told you," wheezed Mr Grimley. "We can't even look after our animals, let alone a ruddy great thing that doesn't belong."

Tom opened his mouth, then closed it again, afraid to ask the Grimleys a question that might be refused. The girls were kneeling on the icy ground. Very gently they began to sweep handfuls of snow from the pterosaur's leathery wings. Tom decided to risk his question. "I'll come and feed Iris," he said, "and the others, if you'll let me?"

The Grimleys looked at each other. Mr Grimley nodded. "Course we will," he rasped. "We've got nothing to hide now. Might as well cut down the hedge as well. Ruddy thing's got out of hand."

"Wow!" cried Tom. "I can climb over the fence again."

Mr Tuttle took the broom from Tom and carefully brushed away the last patches of snow that clung to the pterosaur.

"It's free!" cried Tabitha.

"And fed," said Tom. "The food's all gone."

The pterosaur stretched its neck, opened its beak and "AAAK!" it shrieked.

Everyone jumped back as the creature slowly rolled over and swayed upright. At its full height now, it towered above the two families. Folding its huge wings, it eyed them hungrily.

"I hope it's grateful," Tracy whispered. "I don't want to be its afters."

"I'm scared," whimpered Tulip.

Trying to look calm, Mr Tuttle said, "We'll have to get it up the hill, and then maybe it can take off and fly over the sea."

"Like a hang-glider," said Tom and Tabitha, their spirits lifting.

"How?" asked Tamara, bringing them back to earth.

How indeed? How could they get a thing the size of a small aeroplane to walk up a hill? A thing, what's more, with deadly teeth and terrible talons.

The Tuttles frowned in silence, and then Tom said, "Singing. We'll sing it up the hill. It loves singing. Perhaps it'll follow us."

"Oh, he does love a song," sighed Mrs Grimley.

Without a word, Tamara suddenly ran indoors. She came out with her violin and a biscuit tin. She handed the tin to Tom.

"What's that for?" he said, shaking the empty tin.

"You're part of the Tuttle Band now," said Tamara. "You keep the beat going and we'll do the rest." She began to tune her violin.

CHAPTER NINE

The girls decided to try out their latest number. Tamara had composed the tune, and it soon became obvious that Tracy had written the words. The song was all about food.

> *"Call by, my dear, call soon.*
> *I've made fish pie, my dear,*
> *To eat with a silver spoon."*

Tamara's violin sang across the empty fields. Tom found the beat and pounded the biscuit tin with his fists. No one was about, on that grey Sunday morning, to see the curious procession. Led by Mr Tuttle they marched through the gate, across the road and into the field. Was the pterosaur following? They didn't look back until Mrs Tuttle called, "It isn't working!" As she spoke, the pterosaur's head swivelled round. It glared down at Mrs Tuttle and the Grimleys, who ran back to the front door.

"Keep going," said Tom, not for one moment losing the rhythm.

The girls began the next verse:

"I'll make jam tarts, my dear,
And chocolate hearts, my dear."

Tom glanced over his shoulder. Mrs Grimley was waving frantically. The pterosaur began to move. Its strange clawed feet mounted the wall. It dropped onto the road, waddled across, clawed its way over the hedge and then it was in the field behind them.

"Goodbye, my precious," called Mrs Grimley. "Good luck!"

The Tuttle Band began to climb the hill. On the other side lay the sea; they could feel a damp, salty breeze on their faces. Now there was nothing between the children and the giant creature. One snap of its beak and an arm could be ripped, a head crunched. But as long as they kept singing they would be safe. Perhaps.

I suppose we're being very brave, Tom thought. Especially Tulip, who's usually afraid of everything. All his sisters were singing their hearts out. Even Tilly. Tom felt quite proud.

Above them the drifting snow-white clouds began to glow. Ribbons of fiery light streamed across the sky. The sun was rising.

"Come on, Tuttle Band," called Mr Tuttle. "Nearly there!"

At the top of the hill their father turned and beckoned them on. "Come on. Keep singing. Keep it up, Tom. Well done!"

On came the Tuttle Band, climbing the frosty hill in a strange assortment of clothing: dressing-gowns, woolly hats, wellies and pyjamas. When they reached the wide hilltop they found the sun had thrown a glittering path across the sea. They looked back, still singing, to watch the pterosaur make its last unsteady steps. And then there it was, standing right behind them and staring at the ocean. Did the pterosaur understand what it was, that shining stretch of water? It turned its head from side to side, gazing and gazing.

The Tuttle Band fell silent.

"Look out, children!" cried Mr Tuttle. "Wings coming up!"

The children scattered as the giant wings spread. A warm wind brushed their faces and all at once the pterosaur was in the air. They watched it glide away from them, a strange vast shape that seemed to fill the sky.

"It's beautiful," said Tilly.

"AAAUUUAAAR," called the pterosaur. Not a song exactly, more a cry of happiness. But then beautiful birds don't always sing.

They expected the pterosaur to get smaller and smaller as it sailed towards the far horizon. But it didn't. It was only halfway out to sea when it suddenly vanished. Just like that. As if the sky had swallowed it. As if it had never been.

The Tuttles couldn't believe it. They rubbed their eyes and looked again. The sky was empty.

"It's gone back," Tom murmured.

"Back where?" asked Tamara.

"Into the past," said Tom and his twin.

Was that possible? Tom looked at his father, waiting for him to disagree.

But Mr Tuttle didn't say a word.